THE
MAGICAL
WORLD
OF
FAIRIES

ENCHANTED TALES FROM
FAIRYLAND

THE
MAGICAL
WORLD
OF
FAIRIES

ENCHANTED TALES FROM
FAIRYLAND

Written by
NICOLA BAXTER

Illustrated by
BEVERLIE MANSON

ARMADILLO

5 7 9 10 8 6 4

Published by Armadillo Books
an imprint of
Bookmart Limited
Registered Number 2372865
Trading as Bookmart Limited
Blaby Road
Wigston
Leicestershire
LE18 4SE

ISBN 1-84322-112-8

Produced for Bookmart Limited by Nicola Baxter
PO Box 215
Framingham Earl
Norwich Norfolk NR14 7UR

Designer: Amanda Hawkes
Production designer: Amy Barton
Editor: Sally Delaney
Illustrator: Beverlie Manson/Advocate

Printed in Singapore

CONTENTS

THE TIME
OF BEGINNINGS

When the first tiny green shoots appear above the velvety earth, it is still very cold. Sparkling frost often glitters on cobwebs stretched between dead grasses at the edge of the forest. But those green shoots mean something, and the fairies know it. Although it is not warm enough for their wings to work, and they stay huddled in the sheltered places where they have spent the winter, they know that spring is on its way. And each time that the sun shines palely down, more tiny tendrils push towards the light.

Day by day, the sun becomes warmer. Fairies peep out of their homes and turn their faces to its golden glow. The green shoots have grown, and little buds appear. One day a fairy finds the first snowdrop nodding gently in the breeze and runs to tell her friends.

"Soon she will be here!" she cries. As all fairies know, when the very first flowers of spring appear, the Queen of the Fairies flies around her realm to greet her little people and tell them that the Time of Beginnings has come.

The Queen's first visit this year is to a clearing near the edge of an ancient forest. It is one of the places she loves best. As she looks up at the noble old trees, she remembers that fairies are older still, and their magic goes back to the beginning of everything.

Then the Queen raises her hand, and a tiny fairy plays a silvery tune on a little flute made of reed. At once, all the fairies who live nearby come hurrying to the clearing. They clap their hands with pleasure at the sight of their much-loved leader, and curtsey or bow as they approach her.

"Now, my fairies," says the Queen. "We have all rested during the cold days of winter, but our rest is over. The Time of Beginnings is here, and we must be busy. What news do you have for me?"

The fairies tell her about all the little signs they have seen. They mention the birds with wisps of straw in their mouths, looking for somewhere to build a nest. They tell of the squirrels, mending their untidy drays ready to raise another family. They describe the lively mice and voles, running in and out of holes in the riverbank, getting ready for the new families they will have in a few weeks' time.

"Then you know what to do," says the Queen. "Are you in charge, as usual, Vernal? I will be back when the spring is at its height. Good luck!"

The fairies do know what to do. It is their job to help all the baby creatures come safely into the world. Of course, the babies' mothers and fathers do that, too, but fairies can help in unexpected ways. From dusk until dawn, Vernal sits at the foot of a great oak tree and advises the fairies who bring her news of problems in the wide world.

"There is a little fluffy duckling stuck in the mud at the edge of the lake," reports an anxious little fairy.

"Don't worry," says Vernal. "It happens every year. Her mother will soon pull her out. Grown-up ducks know all about mud!"

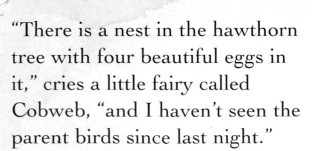

"There is a nest in the hawthorn tree with four beautiful eggs in it," cries a little fairy called Cobweb, "and I haven't seen the parent birds since last night."

"That is a long time," says Vernal. "Find feathers and thistledown to keep those eggs warm until the parents return."

"The wild daffodils at the edge of the wood seem to have no flowers this year," explains Bumble, scurrying into the clearing. "What can we do?"

Vernal sighs. "Sometimes that happens," she says. "Under the ground the flowers for next year are already beginning to form. We just have to be patient."

Then, one morning, Vernal comes out into the wood and feels warm sunlight on her face. She smiles with delight. The little flute summons all the nearby fairies together again.

"My dears," calls Vernal, raising her voice to be heard, "this morning when I came outside, the sun warmed my face and I knew that it was time. You may fly!"

At once there is chattering and laughing from the fairies. It is one of the most exciting days of the year. In the winter, it is too cold for fairies to stretch their wings and fly. They need to open them in the sunshine so that they become bright and strong. Today the air will once again be filled with fairies.

"I'm glad," says Cobweb. "I've been climbing up to check on that birds' nest every day this week. It will be so much easier to fly."

Slowly, the fairies shake out their wings and let the sunshine smooth out the crinkles. Then with a little humming sound, they rise into the air, giggling with pleasure. They wave their arms in the warm breeze and twirl and point their toes. One or two of the little ones try advanced acrobatics and land with a bump on the grassy ground below.

"Come on!" laughs Vernal. "There's still work to do!"

From that day, spring cannot happen fast enough. Leaves rush to unfurl in the forest. Flowers flood the valleys. And in the nests and tiny homes nearby, little squeaking voices are heard as the first babies join the wakening world.

"Don't fairies have babies?" asks Violet, a tiny fairy who has brought a beautiful, broken eggshell to show Vernal.

"Well, fairies live for ever, it seems," says Vernal, "so we don't need to have babies to take over from us. But sometimes, when it feels as if spring is at its height, and the whole world is busy and full of beginnings, a sparkling dewdrop suddenly becomes too beautiful to bear, and a new little fairy apears. That's what happened last year when *you* appeared!"

For the next few days, each time she passes a cobweb glittering with dew, or sees shining drops on a twig or branch, Violet stops and waits, holding her breath. Nothing happens.

Then, early one morning, Violet flies by a wild cherry tree and gasps at the beautiful sight. It has been lightly raining, and little crystal drops still hang among the pale pink flowers. Violet lands gently on a branch to look more closely, and just at that moment, right next to her, the sunlight catches a raindrop and makes it sparkle. With a little silvery sound it vanishes, leaving a tiny, smiling fairy, new to the world.

THE ROYAL FLYING RACE

All through the spring, fairies flit and fairies fly, checking on baby birds, sprinkling raindrops on tiny plants, and clearing away dead leaves so that the sunshine can reach the shy little flowers peeping out beneath trees and hedges. Each day, the weather becomes a little warmer, and all around, the whole world is bursting into life.

One morning, two little fairies meet on a branch high in a noble tree.

"Look out!" calls Bramble. "I'm coming in to land!"

He whizzes down and settles on the branch where a pretty little fairy called Leafe is already sitting.

"Hey, that was good!" laughs Leafe. "Your flying has really improved. Some of us still haven't recovered from the time you bumped into us over the bean field, and we all landed on that manure heap! We were smelly for weeks!"

"I was very young then," says Bramble with dignity. "You can't expect expert flying from a baby. But I've been practising. Look!"

He bounces off the branch and does a full twizzle with wing twist.

"Ah, but can you do this?"
asks Leafe, elegantly swooping
through the air in a figure-of-
eight pattern and performing a
complicated one-leg landing.

The two fairies try to outdo
each other for the rest of the
morning, trying acrobatics and
chasing through the leaves,
but it is only when
they are sitting
breathless on
the branch again that
Bramble has an idea.

"We could have a race!" he cries.

"I'm exhausted," replies Leafe,
"I couldn't possibly race you now."

"I don't mean me,"
says Bramble
impatiently.
"And I don't
mean now."

"Then what in
Fairyland are you
talking about?"
asks Leafe.

Bramble explains that he is thinking of a race for all the fairies. It will take their minds off all the hard work they have been doing recently and be a fun event for everyone.

"It's not a bad idea," Leafe admits, "but it wouldn't be fair, really, would it, if older fairies raced against little ones? And some fairies are, well, *rounder* than others."

"We could have different races for different ages and sizes," says Bramble. "Then it would be fair. Or, the better fliers could start after the little ones, so we all flew in the same race but started at different times."

"That is quite a good idea," Leafe agrees. "Let's tell the others."

Before long, news of the flying race has fluttered around Fairyland. Most fairies think it will be fun. Even the Queen hears of it and, although she doesn't think she will have time to compete herself, she agrees to give the prizes at the end.

"That makes it a *royal* flying race," says Leafe proudly.

On the afternoon agreed, dozens of fairies meet in the clearing in the forest. Not all of them want to race. Some have come to cheer on their friends or watch the presentation at the end. It is all very well organized. The course is around the edge of the forest and back into the glade. The first fairy to touch the trunk of the old oak tree will be the winner, but there will be prizes for runners-up, too.

First, the smallest, youngest fairies line up. "Get ready, flutter and FLY!" cries Azure, who has been appointed Race-Starter.

The little fairies flit off. After five minutes, measured on a dandelion clock, of course, the slightly older fairies also line up.

"Get ready, flutter and FLY!" They're off!

Last of all, the really experienced, fast-flying fairies get ready to set off. They bounce eagerly on their toes, and there are a few false starts before they are finally away.

"They'll catch the little ones easily," says Azure, watching the best fliers disappear.

"I'm not so sure," says a musical voice. The Fairy Queen has arrived. "One or two of those baby fliers are showing real promise. There's a tiny fairy called Primrose who has the speediest little wings I've ever seen."

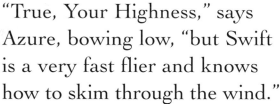

"True, Your Highness," says Azure, bowing low, "but Swift is a very fast flier and knows how to skim through the wind."

The Queen looks up. "Yes, I hadn't noticed that the wind has grown stronger. I do hope all the fairies come back safely." The leaves above begin to rustle more and more, and even quite large branches begin to move.

At last, however, the fairies begin to return. First back is an experienced flier called Barley. It is a while before she can catch her breath. "Swift was ahead of me," she gasps at last, "but little Primrose was even ahead of him. Then, a huge gust of wind swept the tiny fairy up towards the clouds. Swift flew after her, but I haven't seen them since."

One by one, the flying fairies return—all except Swift and Primrose. The Queen looks grave, until a sudden squeal above her makes everyone look up. There is Swift, with Primrose in his arms.

Well, Barley won the race, of course, but everyone agrees that the real winners are the fairies who arrived last of all.

"Swift and Primrose are without doubt our finest fliers," says the Queen, presenting them with crowns of petals and dewdrops. Everyone cheers. "Hip, hip, hooray for Swift, who flies faster than the wind, and for Primrose, who flies faster still!"

THE BUTTERFLY
BABIES

airies are busy in the spring, but as the days lengthen and become warmer, they become even busier. There are simply so many flowers to flit among, checking that the bees are doing their work properly, and more baby creatures are born every day. Looking after little ones is a job that fairies take very seriously. Well, I suppose, they are little themselves. But even fairies sometimes make mistakes…

Young Catkin and his friend Rosebud are very active little fairies. They can't wait to do all the jobs that big fairies do. Sometimes that means they don't listen as carefully as they should to what older fairies say.

Each evening during the spring and summer, as the sun begins to set over the fields and woodland, little groups of fairies gather together so that the more experienced ones can tell youngsters all the important things they need to know. How to tell the difference between a robin's egg and a blackbird's egg, for example. How to help a baby hedgehog who has fallen into a puddle. How to make sure that birds always leave a few berries on a bush so that new plants can grow for the future.

It is all interesting and useful information, and it is lucky that fairies live such a long, long time, because it takes ages to learn everything there is to know about the world of nature.

Catkin and Rosebud certainly have a lot to learn, so they really shouldn't be chatting and giggling together when Silverbark is giving an important talk about butterflies. They hear the bit about butterflies laying eggs, and they half hear Silverbark's wise words about how to be safe when helping a butterfly who likes to land on nettles, but then they are too busy tickling each other and laughing to hear very much at all.

Hawthorn, the fairy who is speaking, looks severely in the direction of the two naughty little fairies and coughs loudly. Catkin and Rosebud behave for about five minutes and then go back to their giggling. In the end, Hawthorn brings the meeting to a close. "No doubt we have all been working very hard," he says kindly, "and some of us, especially the little ones, are tired. It's hard to learn something new when you are sleepy. Tomorrow I will be talking about snails and slugs, and how to help them."

It's a pity that Catkin and Rosebud don't listen more carefully, because the very next day, as they are flying about at the edge of the wood, they spot a beautiful peacock butterfly, sitting on some young nettles.

The two little fairies settle on a nearby branch and watch carefully. The butterfly lazily spreads her wings in the sunshine. She doesn't seem to be in any trouble or to need any help.

"I wish we could find a really grown-up job to do," whispers Catkin. "I'm tired of other fairies thinking we need to be helped all the time."

"So am I," says Rosebud. "Oh, Catkin, look!"

As the beautiful butterfly flaps her wings and flits away, one of the nettle leaves stirs in the wind and shows that underneath she has laid lots and lots of tiny eggs. They are an olive green colour, so they are quite hard to see on the green nettle leaves.

"This is a job for us!" cries Catkin. "Those eggs are going to hatch into baby butterflies. We must make sure they are safe. I expect baby butterflies are a bit like baby fairies. They probably can't fly very well to start with. We'll need to come here every day to look after them."

Catkin and Rosebud are very excited about their butterfly babies. They agree that they will keep their special job a secret. "Otherwise," says Rosebud, "other fairies will take over, and we won't see *our* butterflies fly away!"

Well, the little fairies keep a careful watch on the eggs. It seems as though nothing happens for ages. After a while, the little fairies become bored and only visit very quickly each day to check what is going on. Gradually, even this seems rather boring. One day, Catkin and Rosebud are so busy chasing ladybirds that they don't bother to visit the butterfly eggs at all.

"I don't believe those eggs are ever going to be butterflies," says Rosebud when she remembers. "We'll go tomorrow, though. We wouldn't want to miss anything."

"Something's been puzzline me," says Catkin slowly. "I mean, how is a big butterfly going to fit into one of those tiny eggs?"

"It won't be big, silly!" laughs Rosebud. "It will be tiny. A baby. Then it will grow big."

Catkin still looks puzzled. He is thinking that he has never actually *seen* a small, baby butterfly. But he doesn't say anything. He doesn't want Rosebud to laugh at him.

The next day, the two little fairies fly back to the edge of the wood and settle down on their branch as usual. They glance at the nettle patch and suddenly freeze with horror. Where there had been hundreds of tiny green eggs, there is suddenly a swarming mass of tiny black wriggling things.

"Yeeeuch!" cries Catkin. "What are those?"

But Rosebud has a worse thought. "Oh dear, oh dear," she sobs, "those horrible black things have eaten all the butterfly eggs!"

It seems this must be true. There are no longer any eggs to be seen.

Catkin and Rosebud feel very guilty. "If only we had come yesterday," sniffs Rosebud, "we might have been able to save them. You know, I think this must often happen. I've never actually seen a tiny baby butterfly."

"That's just what I was thinking," says Catkin. "We'll come back when the black squiggly things have gone. There might still be just a few eggs hiding under the leaves."

But although the fairies come back to look several times, the black squiggly things don't go away. They obviously like nettle leaves very, very much and spend their time happily munching through them. As they munch, they get bigger and bigger.

Rosebud and Catkin don't dare to fly too near to the black things. They stay on their branch and watch. Now they are big, the black things have horrible branching spikes on their backs and little white dots on their squiggly bodies.

"I've got another worry," says Catkin one day. He has a lot of worries at the moment, most of them caused because he doesn't really understand what is happening. "Those black things are getting bigger every day. What if they … just keep on growing?"

Rosebud nearly falls off her branch, the idea is so frightening. What if the black monsters grow as big as a squirrel? As big as a cow? As big as an oak tree?

"And it might be all our fault," she whispers. "Those monsters might eat up the whole world … and we let them do it."

"Perhaps we should tell someone," says Catkin, but Rosebud shakes her head. "They'll be so cross," she says. "Please, please, promise me you'll keep our secret." Catkin promises. *He's* worried that the other fairies will be cross, too.

But the squiggly things just keep getting bigger and bigger, until one day, they're not there at all!

"They've escaped!" cries Catkin. "Oh no!"

There are some strange green things hanging from some of the nettles, but the little fairies are too frightened to notice them.

They fly as fast as they can
back to their homes and are
so bothered that they fly
straight into Silverbark
among the trees.

"Ouch!" "Ouf!" "Ow!"

The three fairies pick
themselves up and brush
leaves and twigs from
their wings. Silverbark is
about to give the little ones
a lecture on safe flying, when
he sees their worried faces.

"Whatever is the matter?" he asks.

Then the whole story comes tumbling out. Silverbark asks a lot
of questions. What colour were the eggs? How big were the
black and white things? He doesn't seem very worried.

"But don't you see," sobs Catkin, "they might eat all of us!"

Silverbark smiles. "Come with me," he says. He flies with the
little fairies through the forest and into the fields. He shows them
lots and lots of squiggly things. Some are black, some are green,
some are yellow. All of them are munching and munching.

"They are called caterpillars," Silverbark explains. "The different kinds all like something different to eat. But they do no harm. In fact, they do something rather wonderful."

"But they ate the butterfly's eggs," says Rosebud. "That's awful."

"They didn't eat the eggs," laughs Silverbark. "They hatched out of them!"

"They can't have done!" Catkin is shocked. "Babies look like their mothers and fathers. Caterpillars don't look at all like beautiful butterflies!"

"That is what is so wonderful," Silverbark smiles. "When a caterpillar has grown very big and fat, it changes itself."

"Into a butterfly?"

"No, into a chrysalis. Those green things you saw where the caterpillars had been were chrysalises. They're like little rooms where a wonderful change takes place. But we have to wait."

It is one sunny morning a few weeks later that Catkin and Rosebud sit with Silverbark on their favourite branch and watch something amazing. The green things are almost transparent now. You can see parts of patterns inside. And when one of them begins to split open, a wonderful butterfly crawls out.

"But its wings are all crumpled," cries Rosebud.

"It's just like fairies' wings in the winter," whispers Silverbark. "They have to warm in the sun and stretch out. It doesn't take long. Look!"

As he speaks, the butterfly stretches out its wings, flaps them once or twice, and lifts off into the air. The little fairies are so enchanted that they don't giggle or wriggle at all.

Silverbark looks at their shining faces and smiles. They will be good little fairies one day … quite soon.

THE BLOSSOM BALL

The warm summer sun climbs daily into the
sky, bringing with it the scents and sounds
of long, lazy days. Soon there comes a time
when each day seems to pass from dusk to
dawn without real darkness in between.
On the longest day of the whole year, the
fairies prepare for their midsummer party.
It is called the Blossom Ball.

All fairies love to sing and dance, but the Blossom Ball is special. It is at this party that the little fairies are helped to choose the jobs they will do in the wide world and their final fairy names.

Most little fairies already have a name, of course. It is usually something cuddly and kind that older fairies have chosen for them, such as Bumble or Tinkle. Or it may be based on the way they look. It is not surprising if a pretty little fairy who loves to wear pink is called Rosebud, for example. But at the Blossom Ball, these little fairies have the chance to change or add to their names, and many of them do.

It is a tradition that nothing is done to prepare for the ball until the day itself. There is a good reason for that. Although the ball is usually held on the very longest day of the year, good weather is really important. If summer showers begin in the morning, the Queen announces that the ball will not be held until fine weather comes again. So it is not until the day itself that the fairies begin to get ready.

First there are garlands to be made. Little fairies are sent off to find flowers, always being careful to leave plenty behind, and older fairies use needles borrowed from friendly hedgehogs to join them together into colourful decorations.

Next the food and drink must be assembled. The fairies go to their stores in the hollows of trees and find the ingredients for honey drink and buttercup bread, cowslip cake and pollen pudding. There is stirring and tasting and laughter.

Last comes the most important part of all. Costumes! This is the fairies' carnival time, and they each try to create the most beautiful dresses and the highest hats. They use petals and feathers, berries and seeds, sewn together with cobweb thread. Some fairies wear glittering dewdrops in their hair. Others wrap themselves in thistledown cloaks.

And then there are the sillier costumes. Fairies compete to wear the highest hat. They walk on twig-stilts and pretend to be spiders. They dress up as butterflies, flowers and fruits. Meanwhile, the musicians practise their pieces. Sometimes a nightingale can be persuaded to sing in the branches above.

Everyone is busy and laughing until the moment comes for the ball to begin. Then, as the fairies all gather, some fluttering into the air for a better view, the Queen makes her grand entrance.

Each year, her own costume is more spectacular than the last. A fairy cheer goes up as she takes her place. The ball begins.

It is in the middle of the party, when fairies have rested from their dancing and refreshed themselves with delicious food and drink, that the Queen claps her hands and announces that the Naming is about to begin.

One by one, the smallest
fairies step forward, sometimes
with friends when they are too
shy to speak for themselves.
To each, the Queen kindly
asks the same questions. First
to stand before her today is
Primrose, wearing a
lovely dandelion dress
of yellow and green.

"Ah," says the Queen,
"I know your name already.
You are Primrose, the fastest
little flier in Fairyland."

Primrose blushes and flutters
her wings with excitement.

"I would guess that you would like work that uses your excellent
flying skills," says the Queen. "What will it be?"

"Please, I would like to be a weather-watcher," says Primrose.

The watching fairies nod with approval. Weather-watchers fly around all day, looking for the tiny signs that show a change is on the way. Fairies need to know when a storm is brewing, or if the rain that tiny plants need is going to be delayed.

"And your name?" smiles the Queen. "I'm not sure that Primrose is a very good name for a weather-watcher, or for a famous flier."

"I'd like you to choose," whispers the tiny fairy.

"Then I shall call you Skysinger," says the Queen, "because you will bring the songs of the seasons back to us each day."

Skysinger flutters into the air to show how pleased she is, and a little shower of yellow petals floats around her.

Before long all the smallest fairies have come to the Queen. Some decide to keep their old names. Others choose something new. All go away with smiles on their faces.

At last, only one little fairy is left. She is beautiful, and wears a dress of white daisy petals.

"Please, Your Highness," she says, in answer to the Queen's first question, "I don't yet have any name."

"But what do your friends call when they want you to come to them?" asks the Queen, puzzled.

"They don't need to call," says the little fairy. "Somehow I know without them saying anything when they need me, so I am there before they call."

The Queen looks carefully at the fairy. "Is this true?" she asks. Fairies standing nearby nod that it is.

"And what work would you like to do?" asks the Queen.

"I don't know that either," says the little fairy. "You see, everything is so interesting. I want to know about all the things that fairies do. I want to see everything. Don't make me choose!"

The Queen smiles with tears of joy in her eyes. "Well," she says, "I knew this day would come. You have a great, great deal to learn, little one. And I will not be giving you a name today.

But one day, far in the future, when it is time for me to fly towards the sun, you will be called Queen of the Fairies—the most magical name of all."

Now there really is something to celebrate. As the Queen hugs the Queen-to-be, the other fairies cheer. They know that it will be a long, long time before their Queen is ready to leave them, but the ways of Fairyland will be safe when that day comes.

"To think that I was named on the day the new Queen was found," cries Skysinger. "I will never forget this."

And the fairy choir, which has been huddling behind a tree trunk for the last few minutes, suddenly bursts into song:

Fairies of the earth and sky,
Dance and sing,
Flit and fly.
Follow one,
Follow all,
To this happy Blossom Ball.

Fairies of the night and day,
Twist and twirl,
Laugh and play.
Follow one,
Follow all,
To this happy Blossom Ball.

Fairies of the sea and land,
Fluttering here,
Hand in hand.
Follow one,
Follow all,
To this happy Blossom Ball.

Fairies of the stream and wood,
Greet your Queen,
Wise and good.
Follow one,
Follow all,
To this happy Blossom Ball.

Fairy first, fairy last,
Past and future
Meet at last.
Follow one,
Follow all,
To this happy Blossom Ball.

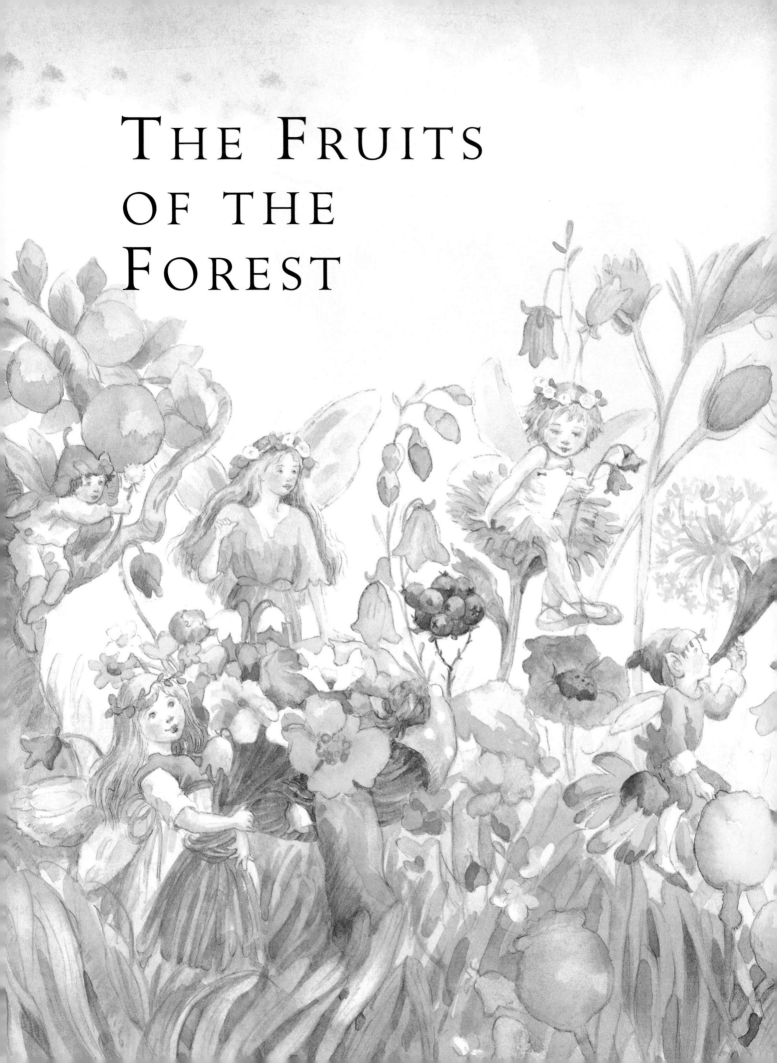

THE FRUITS
OF THE
FOREST

On a warm, soft, summer day, when the golden fields are splashed with poppies, and the apple-tree branches begin to bend with the weight of their shining fruits, the fairies meet to talk about the special time to come. We might call it the harvest, but to the fairies it is and always has been … the Gathering.

Summer is a slow and sleepy time in Fairyland.
Little fairies wander through the flowers,
learning their names and watching how the bees
and butterflies busy themselves among the
bright petals. Older fairies make midsummer
magic, sending sunshine spells to ripen fruit on
trees and in hedgerows. They love to feel the
warm breezes in their hair and sit unseen among
the leaves, watching the little fairies flitting
happily below. As the shadows lengthen on
perfect afternoons, it is impossible to imagine
the dark days of winter.

But nothing stays the same
for ever, and the fairies know
that summer will slowly turn
to autumn. It is time for the fruits
of the forest to be collected, to feed the tiny
creatures of the woodlands and fields during
the long, cold days to come.

And so, one sunny day, the Gathering begins.
Fairies from far and wide come together to plan
this most important time—and to talk about the
party they will have when the hard work is
done. In a glade in the middle of a wood, where
patches of sunlight dapple the mossy floor, fairy
voices, like tiny tinkling bells, are heard.

"Fairies! Attention!" calls a silvery voice, but the chatter of dozens of little people, who are busy greeting friends and relations they have not seen since last year's Gathering, goes on.

"Fairies!" The voice becomes more steely than silvery. One or two fairies look up, but many more are much too busy to notice.

The Fairy Queen signals to a tiny boy in blue, who lifts to his lips a stripy snail's shell and makes an amazingly loud noise.

At once, all is quiet in the glade, except for the buzzing of the honey bees. They never can keep quiet, even for a minute.

"Fairy friends!" cries the Fairy Queen. "We are pleased to see so many of you here today. Later, there will be time for fun and frolics, but now, we have a huge job to do. This year, our task is bigger than ever. The gentle rains and warm sunny days have done their work. Now it is our turn. Have you chosen your teams?"

At once, there is confusion again, as fairies flit
and fly here, there and everywhere. But in a
moment, they are grouped in neat rows and
sitting cross-legged on the ground.

"Fruits and Berries!" calls the
Queen. "Are you ready?"

"We are!" calls a jolly band of fairies
in costumes of purple, blue and red.

"Excellent," replies their
leader. "Now, this year I want
good, quick picking—and *no*
squirting!" The year before,
some smaller fairies discovered
that if they jumped hard on
blackberries and blueberries,
spurts of juice would shoot out
and splash their friends.
It was fantastic fun—
until a Feather Fairy
got hit by mistake
and complained to
the Queen.

"Field Fairies, are you all gathered?"
asks the Queen now, and a host of
golden fairies flutters up. They are
ready to search the fields for the
ripe grains that farmers let fall.

One by one, the Queen names her forces: the copper-coloured crew who bring home nuts and seeds; the pale, floating fairies who gather thistledown and dandelion clocks; the bustling brown workers who tackle the larger items, such as chestnuts and acorns; the speedy, colourful crew who catch the falling leaves that have a special magic if they never touch the ground.

When the gleaners and gatherers are ready, one last group is left. These are recorders, who scratch tiny marks on bark and stones to note the totals of this year's Gathering.

All the fairies turn their pretty faces to the Queen. There is a moment's hush and then, smiling, she claps her little hands. A cloud of fairies hovers for a second in the air—and is gone. The Gathering has begun.

Alone in the glade, the Queen is just about to sit down to plan the Gathering Party, when she hears a tiny sound. A little fairy voice can be heard nearby, muttering sadly. But surely, all the fairies have flown away?

Hidden behind the gnarled root of a tree, the Queen finds a little figure, head in hands.

"My dear," she says, "what is the matter?"

The little fairy jumps and is even more frightened when she realizes who is talking.

"Oh, Your Highness," she says, "I'm so, so sorry."

"But why, my dear?" asks the Queen. "Don't be upset."

The whole story comes tumbling out.

"I was caught in a c-cobweb," says the fairy, "and couldn't get here on time. Now I won't be able to help with the G-G-Gathering. And I'll miss the p-p-party!"

"Nonsense," says the Queen. "I was just wondering who I could find to help me organize things. The others will be tired when they have finished. You are just the fairy I need. Come on … there is lots to do."

For the next few days, while the countryside hums with the sound of fairy wings, the Queen and her little helper prepare the glade. They sew garlands of feathers and flowers to hang from the branches. They talk nicely to the fireflies and glow-worms about making chains of tiny lights among the trees. They make acorn cups and walnut-shell bowls, and scatter petals for fairies to sit on.

"Now," laughs the Queen, "we must talk to the spiders. They make lovely, lacy hammocks for tired fairies to rest in."

"Sp-sp-spiders?" asks her little helper. "Oh, I don't know…."

"Ah, yes, the cobweb, I remember," says the Queen, "but, you know, you'll find that spiders are not so bad."

In fact, the spiders are very kind indeed. When they hear about what happened to the little fairy, they spin a beautiful lacy dress for her to wear at the party.

It is late one afternoon by the time that everything is ready.

"Phew! Now I can rest," sighs the little fairy. But the Queen smiles. "I don't think so!" she says. "Listen!"

The sound of a hundred tiny beating wings fills the air for a second, then there is laughter and singing and chattering on every side. The party has begun!

THE UNINVITED
GUEST

Everyone agrees that this is the best Gathering ever. The little fairies are tired but happy. Grain, nuts, berries and seeds are safely tucked away in hundreds of tiny hiding places. Now it is time to celebrate that one more Gathering has been successfully completed.

As the sun sinks, the fireflies
and glow-worms take up
their positions to light
the perfect party.

There is food and drink for
everyone. Some small fairies
eat so much that they have to
have a nap among the rose
petals. Fairy musicians,
playing reed flutes, acorn
drums, snail-shell horns and
seed-pod shakers, soon have
toes tapping and wings
flapping. If you have never
seen a fairy dance, you have
missed a wonderful sight.

Fairies, you see, dance on
the ground as lightly and
delicately as thistledown,
but they can dance in the
air, too. Their wings
shimmer behind them
as they twirl.

From her throne at the base of a mighty oak tree, the Queen smiles at the pretty sight and thanks each fairy who comes to curtsey or bow before her.

The highlight of any fairy party is always the dance called the Daisy Chain.

Everyone dances it, from the tiniest little fairy to the Queen herself. Holding hands, the fairies form an enormous ring and follow each other in an intricate pattern, dancing in and out, up and down, around and around.

As the Daisy Chain becomes faster and faster, fairies laugh breathlessly, their eyes and cheeks bright with pleasure. Everything is perfect until…

Tooooo! Tooooo! Whoooo
is making this noise?

The deafening voice comes from high in the oak tree. As the fairies flutter to the ground in confusion, a huge bird glides into the glade on silent wings and settles on a low branch. His bright, round eyes shine in the darkness. It is an owl!

Now fairies are gentle people. They try to be friendly to their fellow creatures. But they are often afraid of owls. They know that they are mysterious birds, who fly at night without a single flutter to betray their presence. They know, too, that owls eat other tiny creatures. Their beaks and claws are sharp and swift. It is not surprising that fairies keep their distance.

As usual, it is the Queen who
takes charge. Boldly, she
marches towards the owl
and speaks up in a clear,
courageous voice. "We are
holding our Gathering Party,"
she cries. "It is a tradition
with us. We do not wish
to disturb other creatures.
Pray, whom do I have the
honour of addressing?"

The owl bows his head.
"I am Strix, Madam," he
hoots. "I live in this great tree.
Yooooou understand, the night
is my own time, when I can come
and goooo in peace as I please."

"I am sorry we have troubled you,"
says the Queen of the Fairies.
"We shall be gone by dawn.
In the meantime, won't
you join our party?"

"Noooo," replies Strix more
loudly. "That will not dooo.
Look up! What do you see?"

"Why, nothing," says the
Queen with a frown. "How
strange. The moon has gone!"

"It is covered by a dark cloud, Madam. A huge storm is coming. You and your people could be blown away."

The fairies shiver and hug each other when they hear this news. How can they all find shelter so far from home and in the dark, too? Their fear must show on the Queen's face, as well, for the owl's fierce stare softens a little.

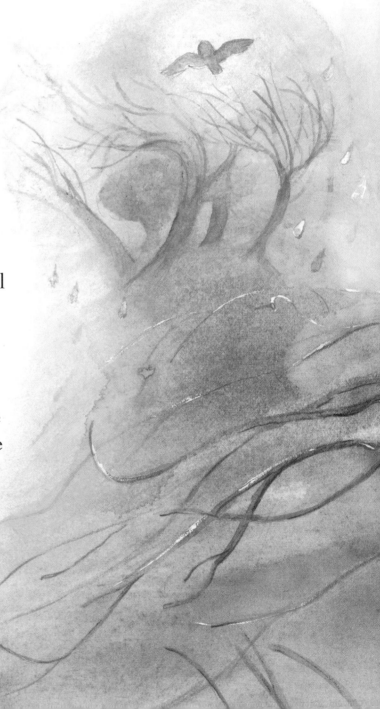

"My tree," he says, "is ancient indeed. It is holloooow. There is plenty of roooom for all of yoooou inside." For a moment, it almost seems as if he smiles. "Nearly roooom," he hoots, "for a party!"

In no time at all, the little fairies clamber and flutter through the hole in the trunk of the old oak tree that the owl shows them. The fireflies and the glow-worms come too, filling the shelter with golden light. In this warm, safe place, the fairy musicians soon strike up a tune, and happy faces are seen once more.

Only the Queen, standing by the opening, sees the ragged

moon appear through the clouds. She watches as
the branches bow before a cold, whipping wind,
and sees the first heavy, drenching drops spoil the
scattered petals the fairies have left behind.

The Queen smiles sadly. It is the same every year.
After the warm, welcoming days of the Gathering,
winter is never far behind. The raindrops are
his messengers, warning that it is time for
all fairies to find their way home.

"Always a little sad, is it not soooo?"
whispers a voice from a
branch high above.

"And happy, too," whispers the
Queen in return. "The seasons
only leave to come again."

"Ah, Madam," sighs the owl,
"soooo true. Soooo true."

A Winter's
Journey

When the cold, dark days of winter come,
there is only one thing for fairies to do.
They find themselves a cosy home and stay
inside until the first signs of spring send them
scurrying out to be busy in the world again. It
is during this cosy time that fairies tell the old
stories of Fairyland and sing the enchanted
songs of long ago.

Finding a safe place to spend the winter is the first thing a fairy thinks about after the fun of the Gathering in autumn. Some fairies like an abandoned bird's nest, lined with soft, warm feathers. Others prefer a hole in a tree, or the nooks and crannies under the gnarled roots of ancient trees. Wherever they choose, fairies make sure that they have friends and family with them. No fairy likes to be alone—for how are the old tales to be told without an audience?

Although fairies prefer not to go outside in the cold weather, other creatures can still be seen in the winter woodland. Bright-eyed birds, in particular, hop about the bare branches. They bring news of the outside world to the fairies and, as they are terrible gossips, soon pass on snippets of information about other fairy groups. And that is how the terrible news of the Queen's illness spread among the little folk.

The Queen herself always spends the winter in a mossy cave on a hillside. It is really just the space made where one boulder has rolled against another, but it makes a grand and comfortable home for the most important fairy of all. Here the Queen is safe and warm in the worst weather, though outside the rain and wind are wild and cold.

But a day comes when the Queen feels that the cold is no longer outside but in her own tiny body. She shivers and coughs and wraps herself in a blanket of thistledown. A heavy sadness comes over her. It is no good. By the evening, the Queen is really ill, and the fairies hovering around her can do nothing to help.

"Tell the others!" a little fairy peeps out from the cave to tell a robin perching above. "We don't know what to do, but perhaps one of the fairy folk will be able to help. Go quickly, please!"

The robin flies off, eager to take his news to all the fairies hidden in the winter world.

Now fairies are hardly ever ill. Living as they do in the open air and the sunlight, with all the good things of the earth to eat, they are usually full of laughter and liveliness. As news of the Queen's illness flies from burrow to nest, all the fairies are worried. They simply do not know what to do.

"Sunshine is what she needs," say several fairies.
"And good spring water."

"There'll be no sunshine this month," another fairy replies, looking up at the leaden skies. "I'd say we're expecting snow and lots of it!"

It is not until a day later that a little fairy called Merrydown hears of the Queen's sickness. "Tell me everything," she begs the bird who brings the news. "Is she pale? Does she have a fever? Is she sleepy?"

The messenger bird tells the fairy everything he knows, but there is a lot he cannot be sure about. Merrydown crawls back into the bird's nest where she is spending the winter with her friends and tells them what she has heard.

"I was thinking," she says, her eyes shining, "of the sunbeam we caught last summer."

"It would be just the thing!" cries her friend Fern. "We will be in the dark," she adds regretfully, "but the Queen should have it. Only how will we get it to her? It's too delicate for a bird with a big, clumsy beak to carry."

Merrydown is determined. "I'll take it," she says. "I know it's a long way, but I can carry it carefully and, anyway, on the way there the sunbeam itself will keep me warm."

The little fairies look up at the ceiling of the nest. Shining above them is something golden, glowing within a lantern made of closely woven cobwebs. One glorious day of sunshine, a few months before, the fairies were lucky enough to catch a sunbeam that shone through the leaves on to the woodland floor. It has kept them warm all winter, but now it is time to give it to someone who needs it more.

So it is that Merrydown sets off on the Great Journey that fairies still speak of. Fairies cannot fly in the winter, when there is no warmth to smooth their wings, so Merrydown has to walk. Even in her cloak of feathers and clutching the sunbeam, she feels the cold.

Merrydown sets out very early one morning, when the grey sky is flushed with pink and orange. She walks without stopping all morning and into the afternoon. It is hard. She has to scramble over rocks and branches without using her wings or her hands, which are carefully holding the sunbeam.

By about two o'clock, her feet are dirty and sore, and the cold is beginning to bite at her tiny toes. Merrydown does not need to think about which direction to take. All fairies can always find their Queen—it is a kind of instinct they have.

Then, just as Merrydown is thinking she must find somewhere to rest, something terrible happens. It begins to snow. Huge, soft flakes come thick and fast out of the sky. It seems darker, and Merrydown now feels the cold trickling down her neck and settling on her head and shoulders. She shivers and stumbles, and, as she does so, she drops the sunbeam!

Paralysed with horror, Merrydown watches the glow bouncing gently down the slope in front of her, leaving no impression on the light covering of snow. With a cry, the little fairy tumbles down the hill after the light, fearing at any moment to see it break on a rock and spill out into the gathering gloom.

But the light rolls on until it drops—*plop*—into a little river at the bottom of the slope. Merrydown gives a wail as she sees it bobbing away in the fast-running water.

"Jump on if you want to catch it!" hisses a voice in her ear. To the fairy's astonishment, a beautiful swan rises up out of the snow, where it has been almost hidden.

Merrydown doesn't have time to think. She jumps on to the bird's white feathers and settles down among them. The dark water rushes them along as the snow continues to fall. At last, as the day grows darker still, Merrydown realizes that the water has become calm. The river has emptied into a large lake, and the sunbeam is bobbing gently on the water only a few inches away.

"You had better stay here tonight," says the swan. "You are so light I can hardly feel you. Sleep on my back, and I will watch the light for you. In the morning, I will set you on the bank and you can go on."

The tired fairy lays down her heavy head and is soon dreaming beneath the night sky. The snow stops falling, and the merest sliver of a silvery moon rises in the sky.

The next day, Merrydown sets off on foot again. She can feel that the Queen is closer now. It has been much quicker to travel by water than by land. At last, reaching the top of a high hill, Merrydown knows that she is very close indeed. Eagerly, she runs forward—and completely loses her footing on the slippery slope. This time, the fairy holds on to the light, clutching it to her as she skids through the snow and comes to a stop … just outside the Queen's winter cave.

Hardly daring to breathe, Merrydown creeps inside. The sunbeam lights up a sad scene. There lies the Queen, pale and still on a bed of swan's down. Around her, the fairy court looks near to tears.

Merrydown doesn't waste a moment. Quickly pulling a leaf curtain across the entrance to the cave, she gently releases the sunbeam. At once, the sunshine in all its brightness springs out into the room, lighting up every corner and bringing a golden glow to the Queen's lovely face.

At once, she opens her eyes and sits up. "Oh, I feel so much better!" she cries. "It's as if the summer has come. Thank you, my dear!" All around, fairies beam and bustle, hurrying to bring food and comforts to their welcome visitor.

It is soon decided that it is too dangerous for Merrydown to make the return journey without the sunbeam, so she stays by the Queen's side for the rest of the winter.

THE SECRETS OF THE SNOW

The snow that begins to fall when Merrydown makes her Great Journey stops only for a little while. Then it begins again and does not cease for a whole week. As far as the eye can see, the world is white. Heavy blankets of snow lie on the branches of the great trees in the wood and bow down the smaller plants. The lakes and ponds are frozen, and only a small trickle of water still flows in the icy streams and rivers. The snow dampens many sounds, so that the world seems strangely quiet and still.

For many weeks, the weather is icy cold. Although the sun shines brightly on the snow by day, there is no thaw. Very few animals venture out. There is nothing for them to eat, and they are better snugly sleeping in their holes and burrows. Only the bright-eyed birds hop around from time to time, leaving their spiky footprints in the snow.

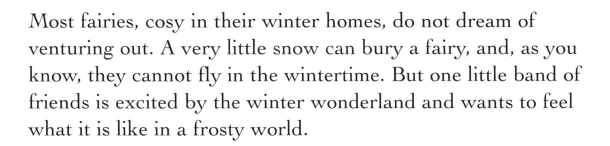

Most fairies, cosy in their winter homes, do not dream of venturing out. A very little snow can bury a fairy, and, as you know, they cannot fly in the wintertime. But one little band of friends is excited by the winter wonderland and wants to feel what it is like in a frosty world.

"As light as they are, fairies can sink into soft snow," warns a Flower Fairy. "You must never go out when the weather is like this. It is far too dangerous."

But to the little fairies, who have not yet been given the tasks they will perform in the outside world, the spring and summer seem a long way away. They want to discover the secrets of nature now. They long to explore the fascinating world outside the old tree trunk in which they live.

One day, the smallest little
fairy of all has an idea.

"It wouldn't be going outside
exactly," he says. "It would be
kind of being inside outside."

"What are you talking about?"
the other fairies laugh. "You're
not making any sense at all,
Shimmer."

But Shimmer knows what he means and he starts to explain.
"Where there's a hole, just at the bottom of the trunk," he says,
"the snow is pushed right up against the tree. This morning, I
touched it and, you know, it's really soft."

"We know *that*," sigh the other little fairies. "So what?"

"You can easily dig it with your hands," replies Shimmer.

Now he has their attention. They look at him with
bright little eyes and start to have Big Ideas.

"So you mean we could dig some away…,"
says Shine.

"And make a sort of tunnel…,"
says Glitter.

"And go adventuring *inside* the snow!"
finishes Sparkle. "Let's do it!"

The little fairies have half an idea that bigger fairies might try to stop them if they know, so they keep quiet about their plan and scuttle down to the roots of the tree where the hole is. Shimmer is quite right. The snow is very easy to dig with their hands, if a little cold. Then Shine makes another discovery.

"You don't really have to dig," she says. "Look, you can sort of push the snow together, so it gets harder. That way, there's no dug-out snow to get rid of."

The others find that she is right, and before the morning is over, they have made quite a long tunnel away from the tree trunk and across the clearing. It isn't very big—just wide enough for a fairy to tiptoe along. And it isn't dark, either, because somehow light from above seems to glow through the snow.

The little fairies just love their new playground. Over the next few days they hollow out more tiny tunnels and even little rooms under the surface of the snow.

Then, one morning, Glitter suddenly falls through a hole into another tunnel! She realizes that she has come round in a circle and found the first tunnel. Now the little fairies can enjoy games of chase all day long.

It is Sparkle who makes the next big discovery. Her tiny hands suddenly touch something rough and warmer than the snow. When she clears more of the white, powdery stuff away, she finds that she has come to another tree trunk. And inside, there is another group of little fairies, who are very surprised indeed to have visitors in the middle of a snowy, blowy winter!

It isn't long before all the fairies in both tree trunks know about what the little fairies have been doing, but they cannot be angry. It is so nice to be able to go visiting through the snow!

Soon there are dozens of tunnels criss-crossing the clearing and travelling further afield, too. The fairies have never had such a festive time, visiting their neighbours, finding treasures in the snow tunnels, and enjoying a whole new wintertime adventure.

"We shall call you the Frost Fairies," the grown-ups tell the little fairies who started it all.

Then, one fine morning, a fairy is walking along the tunnel to visit her friend on the other side of the clearing when something very worrying happens. *Plop!* A big drop of water lands right on her head!

At first, the fairy cannot believe what has happened, but when she touches her hair and looks at her dripping dress, she cannot be in doubt. She runs quickly back to her own tree and calls, "It's raining in the tunnel! What shall we do?"

"Wait a minute," replies an older, wiser fairy. "It can't be raining in the tunnel. It must be something else." And, as they sit thinking, all of them at once suddenly realize what is happening. It's the thaw! The snow is melting!

"Our little ones are in danger!" cries the first fairy. "We must make sure that no one is in the tunnels. They could drown in the drips! There could be puddles! What if the roof of a tunnel collapses while our babies are underneath? Oh, what can we do?"

"We need to sound a fairy warning," says the older, wiser fairy, whose name is Berry. "Where is the snail's shell? Now, find me some big, shiny leaves. Holly would be fine."

Later that afternoon, Berry sets off along the tunnels, wearing on his head an extraordinary hat made of holly leaves. It is a clever idea. If icy water drips on to his head, it slides off the shiny leaves and falls to the floor on either side. And all the time he walks along, Berry blows the snail's-shell bugle. Fairies hurry from the tunnels, knowing that something is wrong.

Soon, everyone is safely at home, and the danger is past.

"We must be careful next year," says Shimmer, "and work out a way to warn other fairies when the tunnels are no longer safe. How sad it is that we won't be able to play in them any more this year."

Berry grins. "Don't be silly," he says. "Don't you realize what this means? The snow is melting! We will be able to go outside again. The world is waking up. It will soon be spring!"

For days, the fairies wait, listening to the *drip! drop!* of snow melting on the branches and the big *schloop!* when a whole branchful of snow slides to the ground. It begins to feel warmer, and one day the snow melts enough for a little weak sunlight to filter through a crack in the trunk and light up the inside.

"Do you think…?" asks Shine.

"Not quite yet," says Berry, but he is smiling.

Then, one morning, the little fairies wake early. At first, they cannot understand why. Then they know. All around them, out in the wide world, birds are singing. From every branch, there comes a busy, twittering, tweeting, joyful sound.

One by one, the fairies creep outside. It is cool still, but the sun is shining, and the birds are fluttering and flirting in the branches.

"Oh, but look," says Glitter. "There is still some snow over there."

"Not snow," smiles Berry. "Snowdrops! The first flowers of spring. Another beautiful year has begun."